EggZactly
The Same

Leah Selig

Illustrated by Susana Josephson

EggZactly The Same

ISBN 978-1-7363614-0-5

"I can't wait for the first day of school!" Hannah screamed. It's going to be so cool!"

We will run bases and make funny faces! We'll trade snacks from our new backpacks, make tongue twisters, and act like sisters!

Hannah planned just what clothes to wear, then dreamed of dancing with a bear!

When morning came, she was so happy! She clapped and sang and was so yappy. "The first day of school is today!" She did three cartwheels and yelled

She went to school, but on the bus,
nobody would sit with her, not even Russ!
   At Recess, at gym class, and even at lunch,
Hannah felt lonely, left out of the bunch.

"**D**o you want to play hopscotch? You can jump first." "No," they said, which made her embarrassed, and that was the worst!

"Do you want a rice ball, it's really delish?" Hannah asked Shayla, Mikie, and Tish. They said, "No, our food is enough, and don't you eat doggies and kitties and stuff?"

"Do you want to read a story with me?" Hannah bravely asked Brittany McGee. She said, "With your eyes, I didn't even think you could see!"

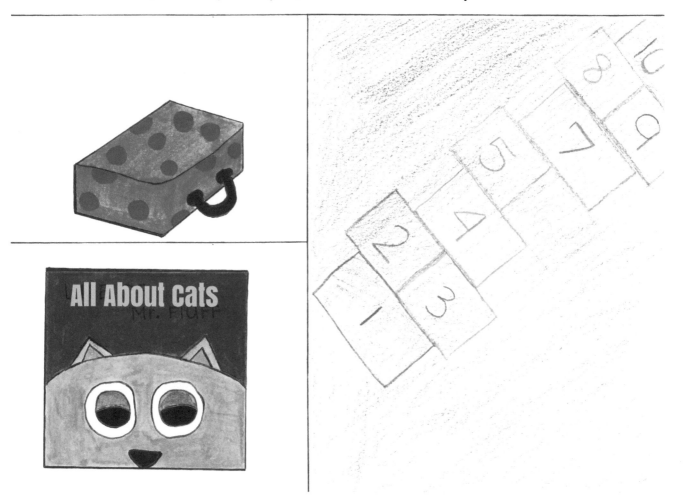

"Hunny, bunny, I see a tear. What happened at school? Is there something you fear?"

"Mummy, Mummy, school was so bad. I don't look like the others, and they made me feel sad."

"They said my Asian eyes do not see and that we eat doggies – we don't, do we?"

"Of course not, sweetie, how awful for you." She thought for a while, then said, "I know just what to do!"

She picked up the phone and quietly said, "Hello, Miss Berry, there is trouble ahead. Kids are left out of the games and the fun – some do not understand that inside we are ONE."

"Hi everyone, welcome to our second day! Before we begin, I have a special game we can play. Here are three eggs, brown, white, and tie-dyed. What do you think they will look like inside? Will they be brown, white, and rainbow? Let's get them open, and then we will know!"

CRACK went the brown, the white, the tie-dyed, and guess what? They all looked the same inside! Everyone was surprised at the teacher's game. Why did the insides all look the same?

"These eggs are like people, like me and like you. Inside we are the same, whether white, green, or blue. We are tall or small – our hair is curly or straight. We have blue, green, or brown eyes, and that's pretty great. We eat different foods and play different games, but deep inside, we're Egg-Zactly the same!

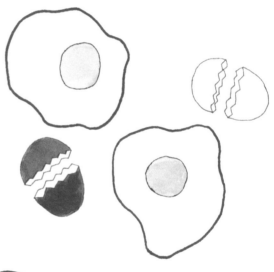

Amazing things happened later that day! "Hannah, want to play jump rope with us?" asked Chrissy and Tish. Jen shared her crayons – they drew a big fish! Ashley saved Hannah a seat on the bus, and they tickled and laughed with that new kid, Russ.

"Hey Hannah Banana, how was your day? You look happy and bouncy, did they let you play?"

"Yes, dad they did! It was magic, I think. Tomorrow, I'll wear my new shoes that are pink! I can't wait for school," I said matter-of-factly.

Dad smiled at mom, and she said "EggZactly."

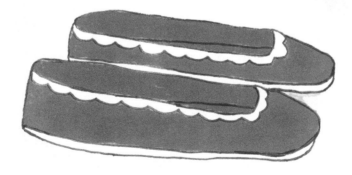

"Thank you, Miss Berry," said Mom, "Your class was a winner. Hannah's friends are even coming to dinner!"

"Oh, I'm so happy," Miss Berry replied. The kids got it, and right away, too, when we cracked the eggs open and saw all that GOO! The eggs looked the same, all slimy and wet, and I have to admit, this was my best class yet!"

We hope that this book helps parents talk with their children about the importance of being kind and including everyone, even if they look, sound, or act differently. We also hope that teachers will read this book to their students and perform the Egg Experiment as one small step toward preventing bullying. To learn more, please visit our website at www.wickedgoodbook.com.

CPSIA information can be obtained
at www.ICGtesting.com
Printed in the USA
LVHW070159080221
678682LV00002B/20

* 9 7 8 1 7 3 6 3 6 1 4 0 5 *